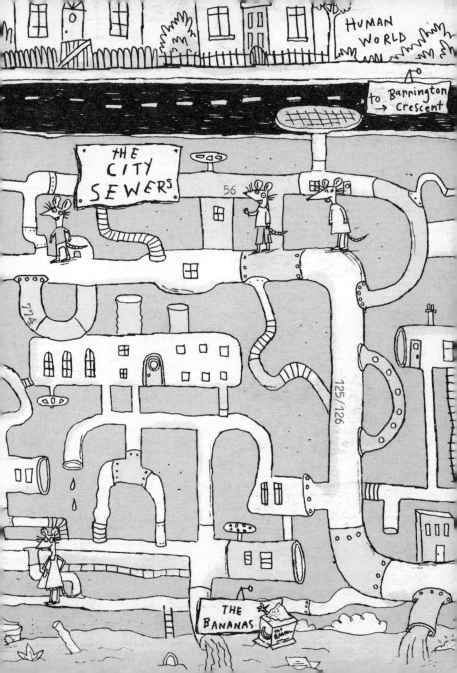

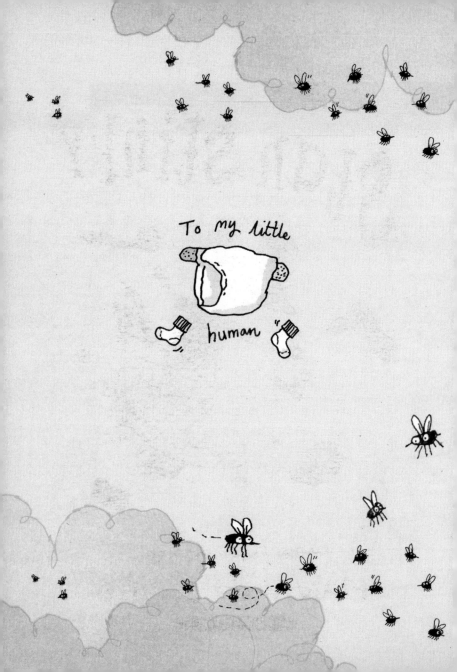

To my little human

Stan Stinky

Written and illustrated by

HANNAH SHAW

⌘SCHOLASTIC

First published in the UK in 2013 by Scholastic Children's Books
An imprint of Scholastic Ltd
Euston House, 24 Eversholt Street
London, NW1 1DB, UK
Registered office: Westfield Road, Southam, Warwickshire, CV47 0RA
SCHOLASTIC and associated logos are trademarks and/or registered
trademarks of Scholastic Inc.

ISBN 978 14071 3624 0

A CIP catalogue record for this book is available from the
British Library.

Printed and bound by CPI Group (UK) Ltd, Croydon, CR0 4YY
Papers used by Scholastic Children's Books are made from
wood grown in sustainable forests.

1 3 5 7 9 10 8 6 4 2

www.scholastic.co.uk/zone

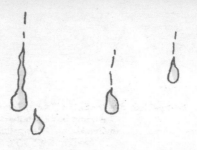

Chapter 1
Stan Stinky Down the Drain

Question: What is this?

Possible answers:

a) Er, it's a drain, of course.

b) It's an entrance to a secret underground world.

c) It leads to someone's bedroom.

The correct answer is . . . all three!

It is a drain, but. . .

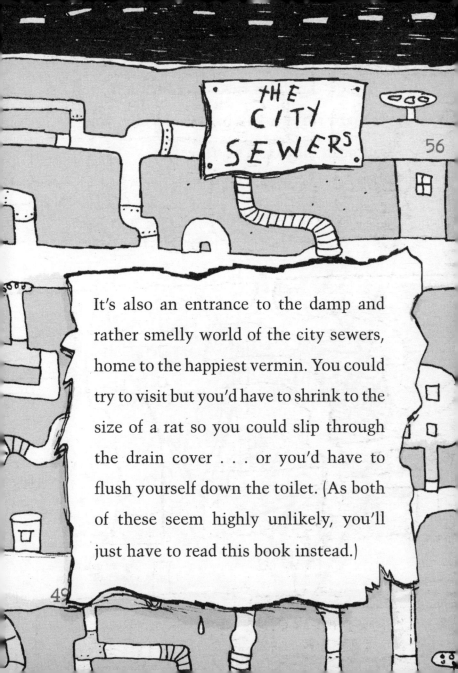

THE CITY SEWERS

It's also an entrance to the damp and rather smelly world of the city sewers, home to the happiest vermin. You could try to visit but you'd have to shrink to the size of a rat so you could slip through the drain cover . . . or you'd have to flush yourself down the toilet. (As both of these seem highly unlikely, you'll just have to read this book instead.)

Inside the drain there is a bedroom, too. At night-time, if you listen carefully, you will hear a little rat snoring, fast asleep in his crisp-packet blanket.

This rat is Stan Stinky!

And on this particular night, Stan was
having a wonderful dream. He was on
a tropical island, surfing a huge wave.
Everyone was cheering, "Go, Stan Stinky!"

Sploosh! The wave broke and Stan
tumbled into the sea. As Stan splashed
around helplessly in the water, he hoped

5

his dream would end very soon. You see, Stan was different from all the other rats. He couldn't swim.

Drip . . . drip . . . drip! Stan woke up.

He opened his eyes. Water was falling on to his head. His bedroom was leaking again. (That was the trouble with sleeping in a drain.)

Stan remembered his dream, sighed deeply, flicked a flea away from his ear and put his head under his crinkly blanket. It was the second day of the rat school holidays but Stan didn't feel like getting out of bed. He was fed up. You only have to read his homework diary to discover why. . .

MY SUMMER by Stan Pipe Stinky

Dear Diary,

My teacher, Mrs Scratchy, has
asked everyone in my class to write
a homework diary.

She gave each of us loads of sheets of
new loo roll to scrawl on and told us it was
"really important to remember all the great
stuff we'd been up to".

The thing is, I don't think I'll want to
remember this summer at all (the most fun
I've had so far is sharpening my pencil to
write this).

It's the end of the first day of my
holiday and I am so, so, soooo bored.
All my school friends have stowed away
on a cruise ship to the Bahamas to go
surfing for the whole summer. And I'm
stuck here, in my drain, with no friends
and nothing to do. Mum said "it was just

too expensive" for a summer trip and I
don't even own a surfboard. It's not Mum's
fault she can't afford to send me surfing.
She works really hard all the time. BUT
it still isn't fair!

She suggested I go and stay with my
mad Uncle Ratts instead. I said, "That would
be totally rubbish." She said, "Well, I'm
sorry to hear that because I've already
told your uncle that you'd like to spend
some time with him" and I said, "He's
loopy, I'm staying here" and she said,
"It's a shame you feel that way
because I'm working every day and you
don't have a choice" and there wasn't
much I could say to that so I shut
myself in my room and wrote this.

Yours miserably, Stan

Stan lay in bed listening to the sounds of human footsteps and car engines overhead. He thought about how he could possibly get out of staying with his uncle. But what else could he do with his summer? The pipes near his drain were usually deserted, as most of his neighbours were quite elderly. And he definitely wasn't allowed out of the drain to explore the streets above, because every rat knows humans are gigantic and dangerous. (At school Stan learnt that humans sometimes kept rats in laboratories and made them glow in the dark!)

A knock on the rusty tin door disturbed his thoughts.

"Stan, are you up?" His mum stuck her head into his room. "You know I mentioned your uncle. . ." She gave Stan a sheepish smile. "Well, he's just turned up to collect you."

"What?!" said Stan, jumping out of bed.

"He's here already?"

Mum shrugged. "Sorry! I honestly didn't know he was coming today. He's asked if you'll go and stay straight away. He says he needs your help sooner rather than later."

Stan's mum started packing his little matchbox suitcase.

"But MUM! I can't possibly go," cried Stan, desperately trying to think of excuses. "I've got all my summer diary to write for homework, and I'll miss my swimming lessons."

Stan knew these weren't good enough reasons for him to stay at home and Mum definitely wouldn't buy them. Swimming lessons were Stan's least favourite activity. Embarrassingly, he still hadn't managed to move up from the baby rat group, where they all wore armbands and squeaked when their tails got wet. The problem was that Stan and his mum lived at drain level, whereas most of his friends lived in pipes much further underground, in towns like Brownwater and Slime-on-the-Sewer. They swam all the time in the flowing sewer rivers, but Stan just couldn't do that.

"You'll have a great summer, I know it," said Mum as she shooed him downstairs. She gave him a big hug goodbye and handed him his suitcase. "Don't forget not to wash," she said lovingly as she pushed him out of the front door.

Chapter 2
The Old Noodle

Stan's uncle was
waiting for him in
the pipe outside.
He was wearing
a bandana and boots
and he was carrying a
drawing-pin sword.

Stan couldn't decide whether he looked like a pirate or a scruffy Robin Hood.

"Hello, my little river-rat," his uncle said, grinning wildly. "Are you ready for an adventure?"

"I guess I am, Uncle Ratts," mumbled Stan, even though he didn't mean it.

"Call me Captain!" winked his uncle. "Everyone else does."

Stan remembered the business card his uncle had once given him:

Mr CAPTAIN Ratts
Municipal Sewer Maintenance
Caretaker & ADVENTURER
The Old Noodle

The bit on the card about his uncle being a caretaker was true – his job was to make sure the sewers were well maintained – but the bit about being an adventurer was definitely made up. Captain Ratts dressed funny, got into all sorts of scrapes and thought he was some sort of superhero . . . and now Stan was going to have to spend the whole summer pretending all this was perfectly normal.

The Captain interrupted Stan's thoughts. "The Old Noodle and Roachy are expecting you," he said, striding briskly down the pipes. "Follow me, young whippersnapper!" Stan hurried after him, not knowing who or what The Old Noodle or Roachy were.

As far as Stan knew, they could be another figment of his uncle's imagination.

After at least an hour of trudging through the twists and turns of rusty pipes that went further and further underground, Stan and his uncle reached the banks of the main sewer river, where they stopped abruptly. The water was brown, fast-flowing and littered with rubbish. There was a large sign that read:

THE RIVER GUNK
THE FINEST (Vilest) UNDERGROUND
SEWER RIVER

"There's my trusty boat," said Captain Ratts, proudly pointing to what appeared to be a floating pile of cardboard and junk.

The Old Noodle was, well . . . old, and like most things in the sewers, looked a bit leaky. It was made from flimsy Chinese takeaway cartons, bits of holey old boxes, and newspaper. It seemed to be held together with string and Sellotape. There was a giant toilet plunger at the helm, and bobbing behind it was a plastic-bottle dinghy.

"All aboard!" declared Captain Ratts.

Stan gulped. He hadn't for one moment believed his uncle was a REAL ship's captain. Although The Old Noodle wasn't much like a REAL ship, and it didn't look particularly safe.

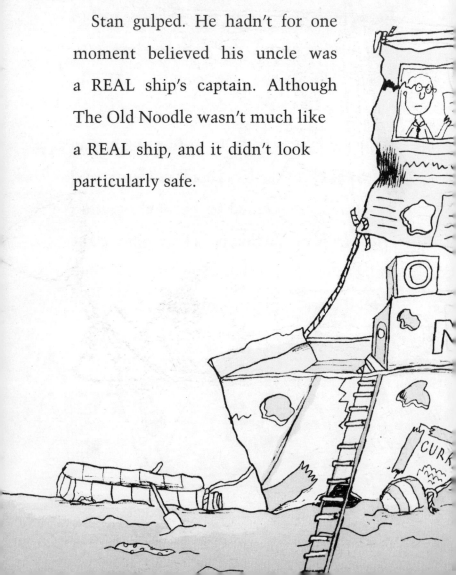

Stan took a deep breath and began to walk nervously up the narrow gangplank. The sewer water swirled and gurgled underneath him. As he clambered on deck, he barely had time to steady himself before he was pounced on by a cockroach with a wooden leg.

"Ahoy!" said the cockroach, revealing a set of rotten teeth. "Roachy at yer service."

Roachy shook Stan's paw enthusiastically with one of his legs, and then offered Stan his next one, and his next one, until he'd offered up all of his legs – including his wooden one – for shaking. "I'm the Captain's sidekick assistant."

"Um, pleased to meet you," said Stan shyly.

Stan was relieved that now he was on board, The Old Noodle seemed slightly sturdier than it had looked from a distance. He followed Roachy, who led him across the deck to a scruffy cabin.

Roachy pushed opened the cabin door and pointed into the gloom. Three hammocks made from orange netting were hanging from the ceiling. "Yer bed," he declared, pointing to the hammock on the right.

Stan's heart lifted. He had never been in a hammock before. It looked kind of fun.

"I think I might just stay in here awhile," he said to Roachy as he unpacked. "Will you tell the Captain I have my, er, homework to do." (Secretly, he was planning on swinging in his hammock first.)

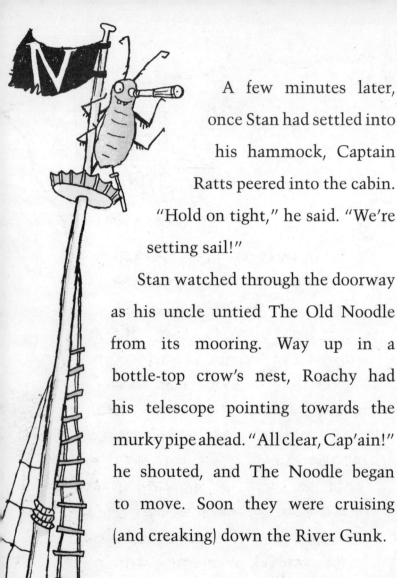

A few minutes later, once Stan had settled into his hammock, Captain Ratts peered into the cabin. "Hold on tight," he said. "We're setting sail!"

Stan watched through the doorway as his uncle untied The Old Noodle from its mooring. Way up in a bottle-top crow's nest, Roachy had his telescope pointing towards the murky pipe ahead. "All clear, Cap'ain!" he shouted, and The Noodle began to move. Soon they were cruising (and creaking) down the River Gunk.

Dear Diary,

Guess what!

I'm in a hammock. They are quite hard to get into but once you're in it's a bit like floating in the air. I'm on my uncle's boat. It's called The Old Noodle. I didn't even know he had a boat. Then again, my uncle is full of surprises. He's totally mad and has asked me to call him Captain. I'm not sure Mum would be happy if she knew I was on a boat because I wouldn't be able to swim if I fell overboard. Roachy the cockroach is currently doing a jig in the crow's nest. I think he's a bit loopy, like my uncle. Humph! The only place I want to be right now is the Bahamas with my friends.

Yours sulkily,

Stan

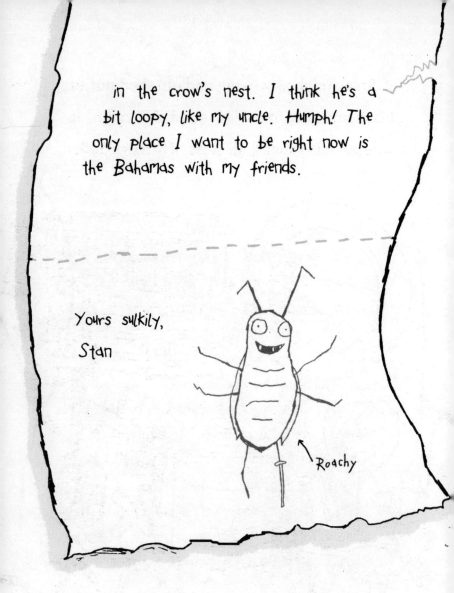

Roachy

Stan finished writing and climbed out of his hammock to look around the cabin. It was piled high with all sorts of strange junk.

On one wall was a big sewer map covered with pins and on another wall was a chart.

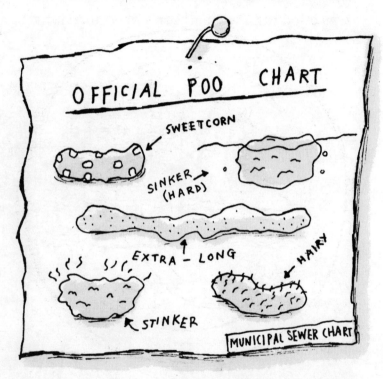

OFFICIAL POO CHART

SWEETCORN

SINKER (HARD)

EXTRA - LONG

HAIRY

STINKER

MUNICIPAL SEWER CHART

Stan was studying the poos and giggling to himself when Captain Ratts' head popped through a porthole. "Many a time I've had to avoid one of those," he winked.

"Look, there's a hairy floater!" He pointed up ahead and grabbed the ship's wheel, swerving just in time to avoid the poo. Stan watched his uncle shooing away the flies and followed him out on to the deck.

"Would you like to have a go at steering her?" Uncle Ratts offered.

Stan was tempted – he'd never driven a boat before, or anything else, for that matter – but then he remembered he really didn't want to be here at all and so he shouldn't try to get involved.

"No thanks."

"Then how about a tour?" Captain Ratts wasn't giving up. Stan followed his uncle around the boat as he was shown all the important gear, buttons and trapdoors.

Trapdoor

Although Stan was officially sulking,  he couldn't help but be just a little impressed.

His uncle patted him on the head. "Don't you go worrying, we'll be doing something exciting soon. We've had many adventures on The Old Noodle recently."

The Captain paused, as if trying to remember something that had happened quite a while back. "Why, it wasn't long ago that we managed to earn quite a hefty reward for rescuing a lady rat from giant leeches in the Swamp Bog of Doom. You see, where there're adventures, there's money, Stan."

Stan rolled his eyes in disbelief. But the Captain frowned at him, so he quickly nodded in agreement, even though he knew from living in the sewers all his life that there was little in the way of adventures.

As if to prove Stan right, the day passed uneventfully as they floated down the River Gunk. That evening, he managed to escape back to the cabin without having to do much. The rocking of The Old Noodle had made him feel quite sleepy, he thought as he lay in his hammock and shut his eyes. . . At least he could still dream about the Bahamas.

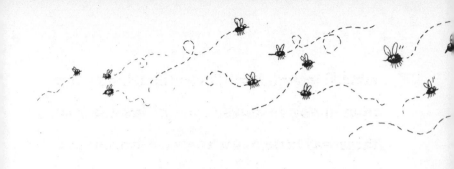

Chapter 3
Desperate Times /
A Rude Awakening

"Aargh!"

"Ouch!"

Stan rubbed his bleary eyes and felt a lump forming on his head. He looked up at his swinging hammock, which had turned itself inside out and dumped him on the floor. Hammock sleeping wasn't as easy as it looked.

Light was pouring through the cabin porthole. Dusting himself off, Stan glanced at a grimy wristwatch that hung on the wall. It was 10.00 a.m. He couldn't believe he'd managed to stay asleep with the boat swaying from side to side.

As Stan got to his feet, his tummy rumbled. He searched the cabin's cupboards until he found one that was piled high with

delicious edible things: mouldy Stilton, gone-off apple rinds, and his favourite breakfast – Cheesy Maggot Pops! Stan sat in the morning glow, munching hungrily on his cereal and slurping the freshly squeezed Slimey Lime juice he'd found. Once he'd finished, he headed out on deck. He couldn't hide in the cabin for ever, he decided.

Captain Ratts and Roachy were talking by the helm and hadn't noticed Stan yet. His uncle was talking in a hushed voice but Roachy obviously didn't understand that he had to whisper back and was shouting loudly. Stan felt bad eavesdropping but it was hard not to overhear.

We've got some sticky poo problems. Just look at it all, stuck to the sides of the pipes.

More seriously, we need money. I tried to keep Stan's spirits up by telling him how many adventures we've been having and what big rewards we've been getting, but really the adventure list is looking emptier than your head.

YUP. NOTHIN' MUCH TO DO, IS THERE? I MISS OUR ADVENTURES... WHAT WAS THAT ABOUT MY HEAD?

39

The Captain forgot all about his whispering and began to pace the deck, grumbling. "Just what are we going to do? No adventures mean no money, The Noodle is falling apart around our ears and we could all do with a holiday! Poor Stan is missing out on his school trip and I want to be able to show him there's fun to be had in this sewer."

Roachy was silent for a moment; then he waved his wooden leg in the air. "We could do ODD jobs, Captain!" he cried, like it was the best idea any cockroach had ever had.

"Oh, festering bog brushes," moaned Uncle Ratts. "I suppose we have no choice. Back to the cleaning, mending and scavenging it is. It's the only way to make money at the moment.

But first we really must fix The Noodle. Only yesterday I found another leak. She needs to be ready for adventuring when the time comes."

Stan didn't know what to think. Sulking about his missed trip now seemed rather selfish. His uncle sounded like he was in real trouble. Stan promised himself he would help out. If he was going to be stuck here all summer, he might as well make himself useful.

He stood up on the wobbly deck and breathed in a big gulp of sewer air.

Was it a bit smellier than usual this morning?

As he approached the Captain and Roachy, they fell silent.

"Ahh! The cabin boy has finally decided to wake up," said the Captain, suddenly sounding cheery. "I'm afraid we have no adventures as such on the list of things to do today . . . or for the rest of this week, actually," he said hastily. "But we do have to fix up The Noodle, and then there are some very exciting odd jobs to do!"

"Well, I'd like to help out," said Stan.

Roachy unrolled a scroll of paper, spat on the back of it and stuck it to the mast.

1. ADVENTURES
To be confirmed

2. NOODLE MAINTENANCE
Things to mend:
Holes in sail
Holes in the hold
Holes in the cabin
Holes in the decking
Holes in the dinghy
Other holes

3. ODD JOBS

"That's an awful lot of holes in one boat," said Stan, wondering how The Old Noodle stayed afloat at all. He read further down the list as Roachy took out a broken old crayon stub and wrote something else on it.

3. ODD JOBS
Mend leak for Mr Scabies in Pipe No. 345
Remove minor blockage for family in Pipe No. 496

4. TREASUr FishiN

"What's Treasur Fishin?" asked Stan, curiously.

"It's a bit like recycling," winked the Captain. "You'll find out soon enough."

Over the next few days, Stan helped his uncle and Roachy mend The Noodle as best they could.

Stan was right. There were AN AWFUL lot of holes. They tried to make things ship-shape, armed with:

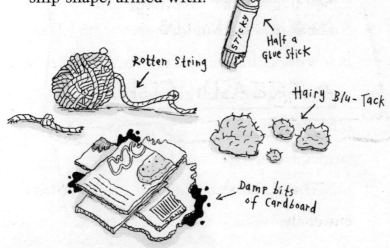

Rotten String

Half a Glue Stick

Hairy Blu-Tack

Damp bits of Cardboard

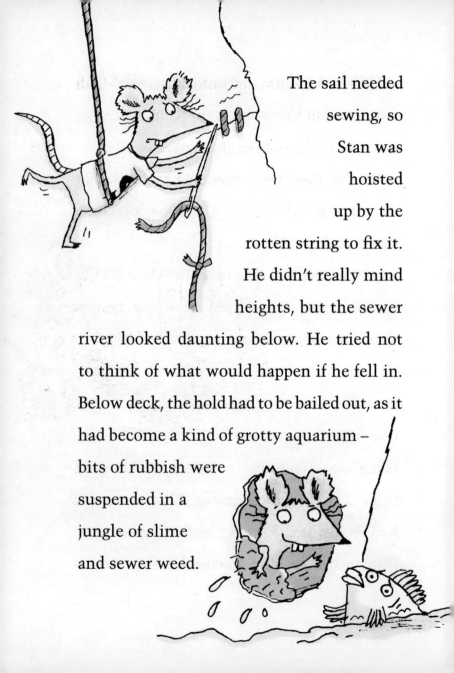

The sail needed
sewing, so
Stan was
hoisted
up by the
rotten string to fix it.
He didn't really mind
heights, but the sewer
river looked daunting below. He tried not
to think of what would happen if he fell in.
Below deck, the hold had to be bailed out, as it
had become a kind of grotty aquarium –
bits of rubbish were
suspended in a
jungle of slime
and sewer weed.

Under the scum, an unfortunate goldfish swam round in circles. Stan patched up the holes and released the poor creature.

Whilst they were mending the holes in the cabin and the decking, Roachy confessed that they were his fault. He had accidentally burnt bits of the boat. He told Stan that before  being an adventurer's assistant, he used to be a chef in a takeaway. The restaurant had been closed down for hygiene reasons but Roachy still loved to practise his flambéing –

maybe a little too much. Apparently, this was one of the reasons he only had five legs.

"I could demonstrate for you?" Roachy offered, sparking a match.

"No!" Captain Ratts cried. "This is a cardboard boat! How many times do I have to remind you that cardboard and fire don't mix?"

After a few days of hard work, The Noodle was still looking old, creaky and dilapidated, but it was a bit less holey than before.

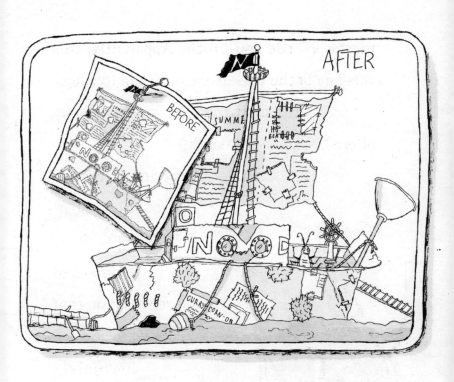

Captain Ratts, Stan and Roachy crossed off the chores with a flourish, and when they got to the end of their "Noodle Maintenance" list, Ratts declared that they were ready to start their odd jobs.

First, they spent a day mending the dripping
pipe at No. 345.

Next, they sailed to Pipe No. 496,

which was near Slime-on-the-Sewer.

A small pipe had become blocked and a family of rats couldn't get into their home.

The Captain assessed the job with a grin on his face. "This is an easy little challenge," he whispered to Stan. "It's good practice for us to do a bit of unblocking. You never know when you might need these skills on a proper adventure. . . Now watch carefully and learn."

Under his uncle's strict orders, Stan disembarked from The Old Noodle and joined the family on the riverbank so he could have a better view.

"RELEASE the PLUNGER!" cried Captain Ratts, dramatically.

Roachy saluted the Captain eagerly and cranked some handles.

The family watched in anticipation. Stan felt just a little excited, too. "Stand well back," he advised. Helping made him feel important.

"FULL SPEED AHEAD!" roared Captain Ratts.

The plunger dropped down from the front
of the boat and moved
into position.
The Noodle
sped towards
the pipe.

The plunger
connected
with the
blockage and
stuck tight.

FULL SPEED
REVERSE!

"FULL SPEED REVERSE!" shouted the captain. The Noodle strained and shook . . . until. . .

The suction broke and the entrance to the pipe was freed once more.

"What caused the blockage?" asked Stan, straining to see. The captain retracted the plunger and Stan and the family gathered round to stare at . . . a sock.

"Tsk," said the Captain, climbing down from The Noodle. "The things

humans flush down their toilets! Don't they realize it has to go somewhere?"

Captain Ratts collected his fee – just one penny. "Happy to help," he smiled, handing the family a business card. "If you hear of any big adventures, you know who to call."

That evening, Stan pretended not to notice
his uncle's disappointment at the one paltry
penny they had earned that week.

"Tomorrow, we must go treasure fishing.
Let's hope we find
some good stuff
to sell," said the
Captain gravely.
Roachy took
out a broken
harmonica
and played
a melancholy tune
whilst Ratts sang along.

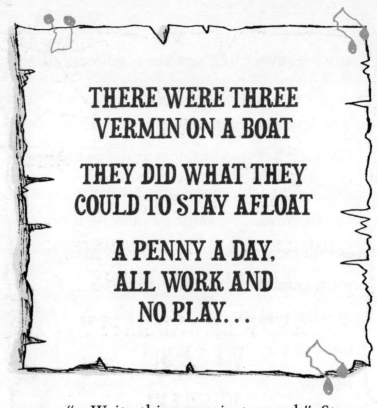

THERE WERE THREE VERMIN ON A BOAT

THEY DID WHAT THEY COULD TO STAY AFLOAT

A PENNY A DAY, ALL WORK AND NO PLAY...

"—Wait, this song is too sad," Stan interrupted. Roachy paused for a second, beamed, and began to change his tune. The rhythm got faster...

Soon they were all singing, jigging and clapping together, and the sound of their laughter echoed down the pipes. The Captain even allowed Roachy to flambé a few maggot droppings (with a large bucket of water nearby, just in case).

At the end of the night, Stan's ears were ringing and his eyes were still dancing with flames.

CAUTION, DEAR READER
Although Roachy likes to play with fire, matches are DANGEROUS and should only be played with by cockroaches, NEVER by children.

Treasure Fishing sounded like good fun. Stan had never done anything like it. They weren't even fishing for fish! They were scavenging for junk that they could sell RECYCLING, as the Captain put it.

Stan helped Roachy get the equipment they needed and then they positioned themselves at the stern of the boat, their legs dangling over the side. Meanwhile, Ratts took the helm and guided them through some of the best scavenging spots.

"The water level seems to be getting lower every day," called Ratts. "Maybe that means it'll be easier to find our treasure."

As it turned out, there was A LOT to fish for in the sewer. Stan could never have imagined the things that came to the surface.

He decided to write about it in his summer diary.

Dear Diary,

Today Roachy and I went Treasure Fishing. We used long poles with big nets attached, which look at bit like this. Uncle Ratts sailed around and we swooped our nets into the water (avoiding the poos, of course!).

At first I didn't catch much, but after a while there was quite a pile of things on deck. I thought they looked more like junk, but Roachy said that some of it might fetch a high price if there was the right buyer in town. BUT who wants to buy a broken toy dinosaur? The Captain explained that one human's rubbish is another rodent's treasure. After a while, all we were fishing out of the river was socks and pants. So we stopped.

Yours sockishly,
Stan.

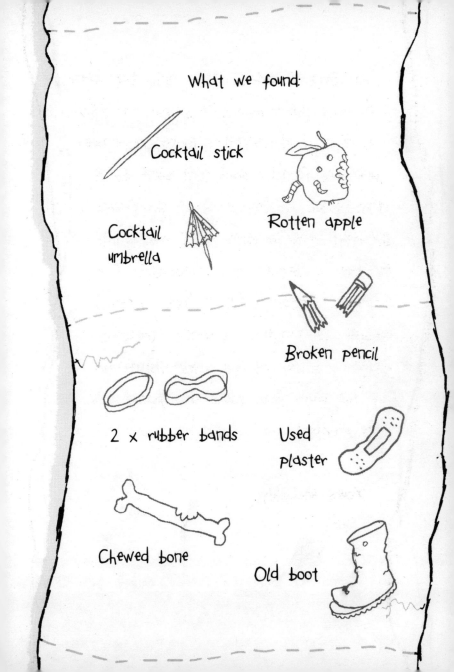

What we found:

Cocktail stick

Rotten apple

Cocktail umbrella

Broken pencil

2 x rubber bands

Used plaster

Chewed bone

Old boot

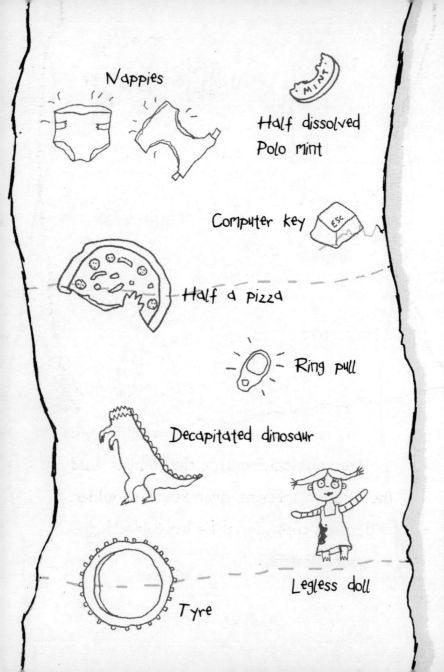

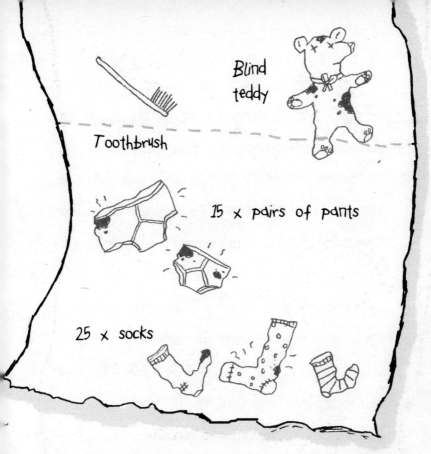

Blind teddy

Toothbrush

15 x pairs of pants

25 x socks

"Are you documenting the items?" said the Captain, peering over Stan's shoulder. "I'll have a copy of that for my cabin ledger. Very nice drawings."

The Captain eyed up the festering pile of stuff, which was already swarming with flies and mosquitos.

"More SOCKS? And how many pairs of pants is that? Very, very strange. I've never seen so much underwear," he pondered. "Hmm." He stared at the pants and a smile spread slowly across his face. "At least we have a use for a pair of these. . . A good day's scavenging and a new sail. Things are certainly starting to look up. Tomorrow we go to town and sell our loot."

Chapter 4
Disaster-on-the-Slime

The next morning, things didn't seem nearly as positive. The water level had dropped so much overnight that The Old Noodle was dragging her cardboard tiller along the bottom of the pipe. It was taking a long time to sail through the sludge.

Stan rarely visited the main town. It was too far down the pipes to walk to by himself. Most of his school friends had homes in Slime-on-the-Sewer and they always made it sound like it was the best place to live. On the occasions he'd been there to help his mum with the shopping, he'd been excited by the hustle and bustle of the place.

Stan had rummaged through the junk in the cabin and found a leaflet for the town, which said it was one of the Top Ten Dirtiest Destinations. He wondered if he'd get to explore properly.

TOURIST GUIDE

WELCOME to SLIME-ON-THE-SEWER

(TWINNED WITH YOU-PONG-TOO)

Nestled on the banks of the River Gunk, the bustling market town of Slime-on-the-Sewer is home to 531 rodent residents; 255 bugs (of different varieties - cockroaches, spiders, dung beetles); an infinite number of flies (which can be big pests - but don't worry, they're harmless!); and one very lost pigeon. The town boasts beautiful architecture in the form of a network of rusting pipes. These are painted in the stunning colours of sludge-green, brown and grey.

ANOTHER BEAUTIFUL DAY IN SLIME-ON-THE-SEWER

HARBOUR

SLIMY LAGOON

Visitors can admire the harbour and the Slimy Lagoon.

The biggest and grandest location is Town Hall Pipe, residence of Slime-on-the-Sewer's beloved Mayor. This is also where the Ancient Sewer Council holds weekly meetings.

MAYOR OUTSIDE TOWN HALL

There are many clubs and societies in the town, including the Society for the Appreciation of Stilton, the Society of Treasure Hunters and the Society of Lost Pigeons (only one member).

A shout made Stan stop reading.

"Blow me down! Not MORE of the blasted things!"

Stan ran out on deck to see what the matter was.

In the distance he could see Slime-on-the-Sewer, but it wasn't getting any closer. The Captain was struggling to steer The Old Noodle back and forth through the shallow water, and the river in front of them was full of UNDERWEAR! Socks, pants and dirty nappies clogged up the waterway. The smell was disgusting, even for a sewer.

"There's nothing for it," said the Captain, "we're going to have to take the plastic bottle – ahem, I mean dinghy. It's going to be much easier to navigate our way through these putrid pants in a smaller boat." Stan thought back to all the holes they had mended. Had they done any repairs to the bottle dinghy? He should really tell his uncle he couldn't swim.

Roachy and the Captain started throwing the treasure junk from yesterday's catch on to the dinghy until there was a great pile in the middle of it. The little boat sank lower into the River Gunk and pools of water started to seep in. Roachy and the Captain jumped on board and beckoned to Stan to do the same. The bottle dinghy was not only holey but completely see-through, and once he'd gingerly stepped in, Stan didn't really feel like he was on a boat at all.

Balanced precariously on top of the wobbling load, Stan clung on tightly as the Captain and Roachy used matchsticks to row slowly forward. They floundered towards Slime-on-the-Sewer. It was a dangerous journey, where Stan almost fell overboard twice and Roachy had to constantly bail out water,

but they eventually neared the harbourside and (with much relief) clambered out.

"Whoa!" cried Stan, as a gust of air smelling worse than a thousand elephant farts assaulted his nostrils. (As Stan's surname suggests, he was used to bad smells, but this one was extreme.)

"This town STINKS!"

And indeed it did. It ponged.

"It's this part of the River Gunk," said the Captain, pointing to the water by the side of the harbour, which was now no more than a trickle of brown sludge. He wrinkled his nose. "This might be the worst I've smelt it."

Whilst trying not to breathe through their noses, Stan, Captain Ratts and Roachy unloaded their wares from the dinghy. They made their way to the market, where Ratts and Roachy set up the stall whilst Stan helped by making some signs. He placed them next to someone else's, which advertised "emergency nose pegs".

EVERYTHING must go. Socks 2 for 1!

Emergency Nose Pegs

THIS WAY

Apart from the nose-peg seller, Stan couldn't help but notice that they were one of the few stalls there.

They waited for customers.

A ball of tumble-slime blew through the virtually empty market. . . Roachy tried busking on his harmonica. . .

Still no one came.

The Captain demonstrated some adventuring skills, which included some flamboyant sword fighting with an invisible enemy. But they didn't sell a thing. The crowds of curious tourists (who usually toured Slime-on-the-Sewer in groups, declaring how "picturesque" it was) were missing and the town's residents didn't seem to be hanging around either. "Oh dear! It's not normally like this." Captain Ratts looked dismayed. "Maybe my swashbuckling performance was a bit overwhelming?"

"More like the disgusting smell is a bit overwhelming," Stan explained, pointing to the stall on the opposite side of the market square. Any potential customers were instead buying pegs to wedge on their noses and rushing back to their pipes, boarding up their windows and locking their doors.

By late afternoon, the town was deserted. The only residents left were the flies. They were having a great time. In fact, they were having a party. "Buzz off!" shouted the Captain angrily, batting them out of the way. It really had been a disastrous day. They hadn't sold a thing.

The smell had become so unbearable (it was now worse than *ten* thousand elephant farts) that Captain Ratts decided to spend the one penny they had earned on pegs. Roachy didn't have a nose so he wore his over his sensitive antenna.

"Dat's bedder," said Stan, even if it did pinch a bit. Roachy started packing up their unsold wares.

"Dime do head off," huffed Captain Ratts.

They all traipsed back to the dinghy, which had to be hauled out of the sludge.

The Captain took one look at the clogged river and made a decision that they were all too tired to face the journey back to The Noodle. Roachy smiled and said that his five and a half legs "might've fallen off" if he'd had to do any more bailing. Stan was relieved, too. He didn't fancy being stuck on the river in the dark.

Together they turned

the dinghy over to make a kind of tent. It wasn't nearly as comfortable as relaxing in a hammock. The Captain sat under it looking miserable, whilst Roachy tried to catch flies to eat – with little success.

The only moment of excitement was when a nervous postal fly cycled by to deliver a postcard. It was for Stan from his friends.

BAHAMAS

• CARTE POSTALE • POST CARD

Dear Stan,

Happy holidays! We have just got to the Bahamas after a long stow-away cruise. There were so many rats on board but plenty of food to go round. Pete Plops fell into the chocolate fountain and almost got caught by a Human. GULP! He escaped by hiding under a pineapple. We've been practising our surfing today. There are some BIG waves and lots of rainbow fish. You should see Fiona Fleabag's sunburn! She fell asleep and burnt her tail bright pink. Hope you're having a great time back home.

From all the rat gang!

P.S. We're all too busy to write our homework diaries. Mrs Scratchy is going to go MAD!

Stan Stinky

C/O Captain Rat

The Sewers

Via Fly Post

← Fiona!

Well, at least I've got time to write my diary, thought Stan, sharpening his pencil.

But as the light began to fade, fumes of disgusting gases rose off the river and began to seep into their makeshift shelter. Stan blinked. He couldn't see to write. The smog was so thick that he could barely focus on the nose peg in front of his face. He could just make out the form of Captain Ratts, slumped glumly in the corner, whilst next to him Roachy yawned widely (the whiff of his breath was almost as bad as the yellow smog!). Stan put down his pencil and—

PARP! PAAAARRRP!

A fog horn bellowed from the Town Hall.

"This is the Mayor speaking – would all residents please come to the Town Hall immediately? An emergency crisis meeting is now in progress!"

The Captain leapt to his feet as if he'd been stung by a wasp and immediately rushed off, leaving Roachy and Stan to dash after him. "Wait for us," called Stan, but Captain Ratts was already halfway down the main street. They ran to catch him up.

Chapter 5
A Crisis Meeting
(Meeting Crisis!)

The Town Hall was jam-packed with rats and bugs of every description, either holding their noses or sporting nose pegs. Stan tried to stay close to his uncle as they pushed through the crowds. It seemed like everyone knew the Captain in Slime-on-the-Sewer. They nodded and waved at him as he passed. The Captain doffed his peg like it was a hat and greeted them all as if they were long-lost friends. "Hello, erm . . . Mr Crud, sir. How is business?" "Good to see you, Waxy, old chap." "Looking dashing as always, Miss Gappy-Teeth." Roachy followed behind, his usual manic grin plastered from antenna to antenna. Eventually, Stan, Ratts and Roachy found themselves in front of a podium. Stan stared up in awe. The Town Hall was the biggest pipe building he'd ever been in. The ceiling was decorated with gold bottle tops, and between the copper plumbing, paintings of famous past residents covered the walls. Columns rose up high above the masses, with statues on top of them.

A trumpet sounded and the room fell silent. "The Mayor is coming!" shouted a voice. A large rotund rat wearing a long green cloak strode on to the podium. Around his neck swung a big gold letter "M" for Mayor. He stopped and bowed to the audience, showing off a sparkling silver nose peg. Behind him the Ancient Sewer Council – a number of old rats and beetles – shuffled in. The Captain pointed them out to Stan. "They make all the important decisions around here," he muttered.

The Mayor looked very seriously at the crowd and cleared his throat. "Residunts, frrriends an' fellow Slime-on-der-Sewerites, we are gaddered 'ere doday—"

"We can't under-tand a ding back 'ere," shouted a rat.

"Dy dear fellow, spick up," the Mayor said, not understanding the speaker.

This is hopeless, thought Stan. He freed his nose and tested the air. It didn't smell too bad inside Town Hall Pipe. He bravely called out, "I think we might hear each other better if we all took our pegs off."

The Mayor frowned. "Whad was dat?"

"Remove your peg, sir," a beetle whispered loudly into his ear. The Mayor slowly unpegged his nose, took a little sniff, and smiled. "What a sensible young rat," he declared. "Now everyone can understand me. Where was I? Our glorious town is under threat. As you know, we sewer dwellers love a bit of dirt and stinkiness, but this is too much! The smell, the smog and the germs have made Slime-on-the-Sewer almost uninhabitable. Something needs to be done. Our beloved River Gunk is full of pants and socks. But why? And how do we stop it? Anyone who is able to answer either of these two questions will be rewarded generously . . . with TWO GOLD TAPS!"

The Mayor took out a large poster and pinned it to the wall.

There were murmurs all round.

"Firstly, does anyone have any ideas about what is causing our overflowing underwear problem?" began the Mayor. Paws and hairy legs shot up around the room. Two gold taps was a handsome reward.

One by one, eager residents came up to explain their theories to the Mayor and the Ancient Sewer Council.

These ranged from the ridiculous to . . . the even more ridiculous.

"An underwear factory exploded."

"Humans are worried about rats' modesty and are trying to dress them."

"A sock monster is lurking deep in the sewers and is trying to attack the town."

All through the explanations, Captain Ratts had been shaking his head. "If I may, Mayor. . ." he boomed, and jumped up on to the podium.

"These theories are, er, interesting, but aren't we forgetting something?"

The Mayor looked taken aback. "Do continue, Captain."

Stan watched his uncle puff up his chest. He was in his element.

"Gentlefolk of Slime-on-the-Sewer, we are rushing ahead of ourselves. The issue

is not *why* the socks and pants are here or *how* they arrived, the issue is *what they have done* now they're here. The underwear has clogged the river and now the water level in the River Gunk is low. This is why the smell has got so bad. Ladies and gentlerats, we have a GIANT BLOCKAGE!"

There was more excited chatter. Very rarely did the River Gunk get blocked.

"Of course," the Captain continued, "we must UNBLOCK the blockage but also discover where these pesky pants and socks are coming from. . . And for that we need an experienced sewer technician with the correct equipment and a strong head for adventures. Namely . . . myself –" he paused as if forgetting something "– and of course my trusted team." He gestured to Stan and Roachy, winking at them. Stan's mouth dropped open at the Captain's shameless self-promotion, but he winked back.

"Well," the Mayor said thoughtfully. "If you think you can find out what's causing this crisis AND solve it, then you're the rat for the job. We're expecting great things of you, Captain. Don't let us down."

"I promise to save Slime-on-the-Sewer from a smell worse than death," Captain Ratts replied.

"Hurray!" cheered the crowd.

The hopeful residents replaced their nose pegs, filed out of the doors and went straight back to the safety of their homes.

Alone in the Town Hall with his uncle and Roachy, Stan began to understand the enormousness of what the Captain had volunteered them for. But the Captain didn't seem worried. Instead, he was incredibly overexcited. He and Roachy were hopping up and down like crickets.

Captain Ratts grabbed Stan and gave him a bear hug. "An ADVENTURE! A proper adventure AT LAST!"

"And don't forget the prize, Captain!" Roachy lovingly stroked the reward poster with the gold taps on.

"Rightio," Captain Ratts replied, manning the flip chart (ripping off what looked like important pages of meeting notes and chucking them in the bin). "Let's brainstorm ideas of how we are going to pull this one off!"

Dear Diary,

We are finally back on The Old Noodle after another nail-biting bottle-dinghy journey. Last night we came up with a "plan of action". Here's the plan:

1. Find blockage of underwear.
2. Find where underwear is coming from.
3. Stop underwear appearing.
4. Unblock blockage.
5. Save the day.

I suggested that we needed to have a bit more detail in our plan, but the Captain insisted it wouldn't be an adventure if we knew what was going to happen. We're hoping to find the blockage as soon

as we can. We've already been trying
to clear a path for The Old Noodle
through the River Gunk - although I'm
sure I could hear the bottom of the boat
dragging along the pipe. My uncle would
normally be worried about such things, but
both he and Roachy are so happy to be
adventuring, they haven't paid the slightest
bit of notice. I'm trying to be excited, too
but I can't help but feel a little jittery.
I've got my paws crossed nothing else
will go wrong!

Yours - jittering like a jitterbug,

Stan

Chapter 6
The Gigantic Mountain of Underwear

The journey to find the blockage was proving difficult and slow. With Slime-on-the-Sewer far behind them, Stan knew that there was no going back now. They were heading straight towards where the pants and socks were thickest, and the River Gunk was becoming less and less like watery sludge (which was bad enough) and more like nasty treacle.

Even if they had wanted to turn round,
the water was too shallow to do so.

As for the smelly
germ smog, it was even
worse than before. The thick cloud
surrounded them so that they were reduced
to zero visibility. They were sailing blind.
Ratts, Roachy and Stan had given up on the
clothes pegs because they were finding it
hard to breathe with them on. Roachy had
taken to trying to hoover up the smog but
this really wasn't working. Let's hope we
find this blockage soon, thought Stan as he
fished another pair of putrid pants out of the
path of The Old Noodle.

"The blockage must be close," said the Captain, optimistically. He was squinting into the stinky gloom as if he could sense something coming. And then. . .

Flump!

The Old Noodle had hit something very large and soft. Its front crumpled a little. Stan lost his balance and clung to the mast to stop himself toppling overboard.

"This must be it," called Roachy from his vantage point, even though he couldn't see anything either. "Just think, Cap'ain, those goldy taps are almost in our grasp."

He rubbed his legs together with glee.

The Captain fumbled around in the cabin mumbling, "I know we have a light somewhere." He started pressing random buttons. The Old Noodle blasted its horn—

PARP-
POOP!

"Oops. Wrong one."

CLUNK... Buzzzzz!

"Found it!"

The Captain pressed a large button. A dusty light bulb emerged from a trapdoor. It was hoisted up the mast on the end of a long wire by squeaky cogs and pulleys.

Suddenly everything was illuminated. Stan stared through the swirling smog and into the pipe ahead, except there was no pipe ahead. Instead there was the most enormous pile of pants and socks Stan had ever seen.

It filled the entire pipe and towered higher than the tallest building in Slime-on-the-Sewer. It was

A MOUNTAIN OF UNDERWEAR.

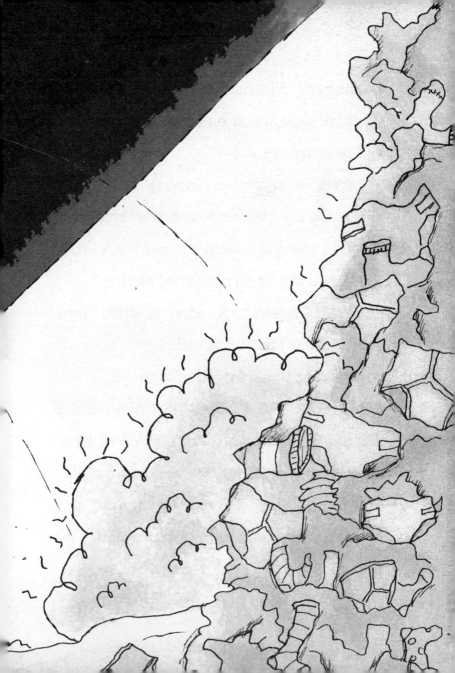

"Burping bluebottles!" yelped Roachy. They all stood open-mouthed and stared at the monstrosity.

"Well, what are we waiting for?" cried the Captain. "We've found our blockage! Let's get to work. Roachy, reverse just a little. We need a run-up to get a good plunge."

"Yes, Cap'ain." Roachy scuttled into position and The Old Noodle began to creak towards the underwear mountain.

"LOWER THE PLUNGER!" shouted the Captain to Stan, who was thrilled to have such an important job. He yanked a handle.

The plunger pushed up against the blockage and . . . nothing happened. Try as they might, they couldn't get a firm suction.

The blockage was just too soft.

They tried again, but this time the plunger sank even deeper into the wet, mouldy pants and . . . disappeared!

"REVERSE! REVERSE!" flapped the Captain. Roachy tried to crank the reverse lever back as hard as he could. But the plunger was well and truly stuck.

"Let's give it some welly!" cried Captain Ratts, as he kicked the lever hard.

The Old Noodle shook and strained, and then it shot backwards.

The plunger had broken clean off. Only a splintered piece of wood remained.

"Alas," said Ratts, "the pant pile has eaten the plunger. That's blown it! Stan! Where's that plan?"

Stan took out their adventure plan:

1. Find blockage of underwear.
2. Find where underwear is coming from.
3. Stop underwear appearing.
4. Unblock blockage.
5. Save the day.

"That's why we goofed up, Cap'ain," said Roachy. "We did the wrong thing first. We never found where these pants and things are coming from."

"Yes," agreed the Captain, "but in order to find the cause of the blockage, we need to get to the other side, so we need to . . . unblock it." He sounded uncertain.

The Captain took out an old sewer map and began to puzzle over it. He labelled the underwear mountain with a cross.

"Hmm, it looks like this blockage is right near the waste outlet for Pipe No. 567, and if my calculations are correct, we need to find the entrance to . . . yes, that's it! We need to follow this pipe here, which leads to a . . . which is . . . ah, here."

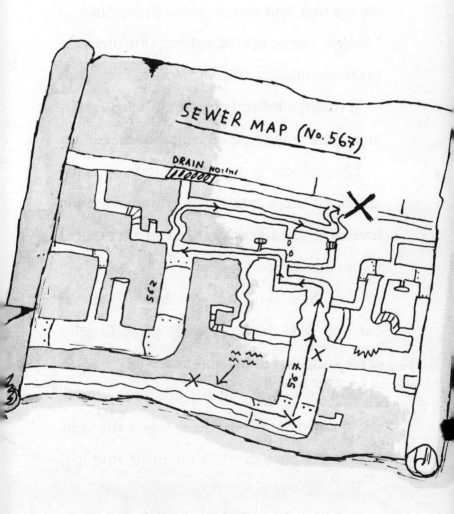

Captain Ratts scribbled another big **X** on the map and furrowed his brow. "Just as I feared, the only pipe behind this blockage takes us into . . . a human house."

Stan gasped. Surely his uncle wasn't going to suggest going near anything so dangerous.

"Ah, no use being lily-livered about it," chuckled the Captain. "A trip above drain level will add a little bit of extra excitement to our adventure."

"But how will we get there when we can't get past the blockage?" asked Roachy, scratching one of his antenna.

Stan looked up and gulped. At the top of the massive pant pile there was a tiny gap. Was it big enough for a rat to fit through?

Would his uncle be mad enough to try?

Nervously, he pointed it out.

"Well done, Stan! We can squeeze through to the other side," beamed the Captain. "We'll just have to climb to the top of Underwear Mountain! Roachy, you know what we need. . ."

Roachy scurried off and came back with two bulging bags.

"Our adventure suits!" proclaimed the Captain, smiling. "How wonderful to be able to wear them again."

Stan watched as the Captain and Roachy zipped, clipped and squeezed themselves into their extraordinary outfits.

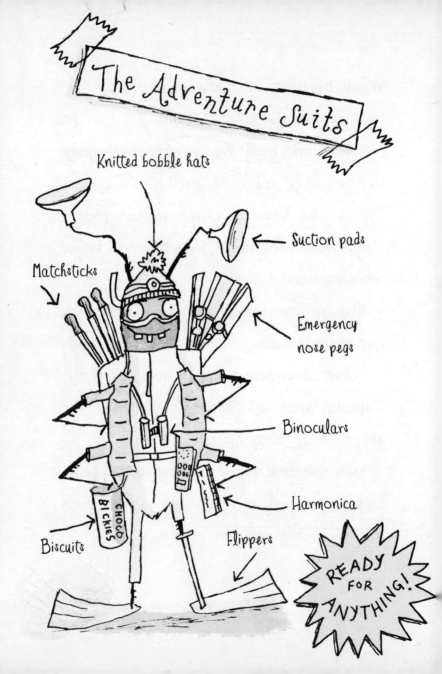

Head lamps

Goggles

Telescope

Batteries

Life jackets

Underwater
pocket watch

Rope with
claw

Wetsuits

Walkie-talkies

"How do we look?" said Ratts, doing a jig so his gear jangled.

Stan giggled. "Very . . . um . . . professional. Is there an outfit for me?"

Roachy looked confused. The Captain looked down at his flippers. "I'm sorry, Stan. You can't come. It's just too dangerous. We don't know what we'll find up there and your mum would be furious with me if I didn't deliver you back in one piece."

Stan was both relieved and disappointed. He wanted to be a part of the action, but he was terrified of humans.

"You're an important member of our adventure team," said Captain Ratts. "We need someone to take care of The Old Noodle and wait for our return. You can listen out for our radio contact." He patted Stan fondly on the head.

Stan instantly felt better. Looking after The Noodle was a big responsibility.

Using a catapult, Roachy fired up the rope with the claw and it attached itself to the top of the pile. Stan watched with a mixture of envy and awe as Roachy and the Captain scaled the mountain of underwear. Together they climbed higher and higher until they

looked like tiny specks. Stan clambered up the mast and angled the light bulb like a spotlight through the smog so he could see where they were going. Eventually they vanished over the top.

"Goodbye," said Stan, to himself.

He stood out on deck for a while, listening to the sound of buzzing mosquitos.

Then, through the cabin window he spotted the map. They'd forgotten it!

He went into the cabin and tried to radio his uncle.

"This is STAN. You've forgotten your MAP. OVER."

There was a crackle on the other end.

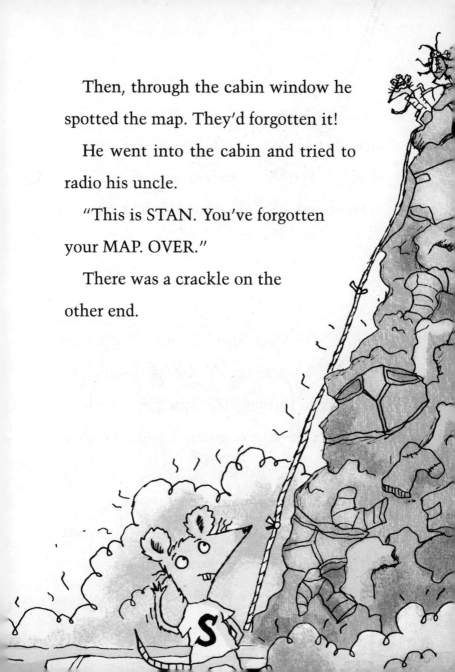

"Hello?" called Stan. "Are you there? OVER." Stan heard a splash over the airwaves . . . and a strange gurgling noise, then NOTHING. The radio cut off.

He stared out of the porthole and waited. . .

. . .and waited

. . .and waited.

He thought about the dangerous humans and hoped Ratts and Roachy were all right. He knew they had been on adventures before, but had any been as daredevil as this? What if they'd got lost without their map?

Stan gazed up at the towering mountain. Dangling down the side was the rope that the Captain and Roachy had used to climb it.

Could he?

Should he?

Yes! He HAD to go and find them. The Captain and Roachy **needed his help!**

Chapter 7
In Deep Water

Stan grabbed a rucksack and searched The Old Noodle for anything that might come in useful on his journey. He certainly wasn't going to be as well equipped as his uncle and Roachy, but this was an emergency, and there was no time to lose.

In his bag, he put:

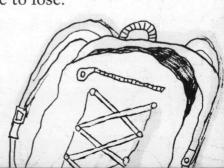

His diary and pencil in case he needed to record the events

String/rope

A cheese-rind snack

His uncle's map

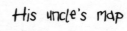

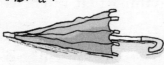

An umbrella

He slipped on a pair of wellington boots and, feeling full of courage, he took a great big LEAP at the dangling rope . . . and fell flat on his face.

"Yowch!"

Stan wasn't sure he was cut out for this adventuring malarkey. He dusted himself off and leapt again. This time he managed to catch the rope firmly between his paws. He heaved himself up and up, climbing higher than he'd ever climbed before. Down below, The Old Noodle looked small and battered, and its outline was blurry through the swirling yellow clouds of germs. It wasn't long before it disappeared from view. Stan was scarily high up, but he just had to think of his uncle and Roachy and he felt able to keep going.

With one last scrabble, he reached the end of the rope. His ears brushed along the top of the sewer pipe as he clung to the mouldy underwear at the peak. He breathed in, then squeezed himself through the gap his companions had disappeared into earlier.

SQUELCH, SQUELCH!

He wriggled forward into the soft folds of a grubby nappy. There didn't seem to be any end to the blockage. Stan panicked for a moment, convinced he was going to be

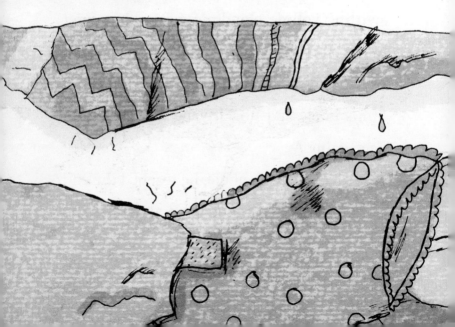

stuck at the top of the pipe for ever. But he couldn't turn back now. He'd come this far. . . And then, with his next wriggle, he found himself poking out of the end of a holey sock. Finally he could breathe fresh sewer air. He was on the other side of the mountain!

Below him, he saw his own reflection. The water on this side of the blockage lapped at his wellingtons. It was as deep as the underwear mountain was tall.

"Yikes," gulped Stan.

He rummaged in his rucksack and checked his uncle's map. It wasn't good news. The route that Ratts had marked showed Stan that he had to get to a pipe on the other side of the one he was in. It was too far to jump. He would have to swim!

Stan remembered his last proper swimming lesson. He had been wearing armbands, a rubber ring and flippers. "Kick your legs," the instructor had cried. But Stan had panicked and sunk. Now, staring at the bottomless expanse of brown water in front of him, he wished he'd tried harder. If he had, maybe he wouldn't be here at all; he'd be learning to surf in the Bahamas.

But he wasn't in a swimming lesson now. Ratts and Roachy might be in danger. He had to think of a way to get across.

Opening his rucksack, he took the cheese rind out and chewed on it whilst contemplating his fate. He looked through everything he'd brought for anything that might help, tipping his rucksack upside down. As he did so, the umbrella fell out and sprang open as it tumbled into the water. *Sploosh!*

Oh well, thought Stan as it bobbed about, what use is an umbrella in a sewer, anyway?

But . . . the umbrella didn't sink. In fact, it floated rather nicely. Like a boat.

It gently twirled a little further away. He didn't have long!

Stan kicked off his wellies, squeezed his eyes shut, held on to his tail and JUMPED IN! He splashed about frantically as he tried to grab the umbrella's edge. Feeling it in his paws, he held on tight, keeping his whiskers above water.

"I'm floating!" he shouted, although no one was around to hear him. He kicked his legs out behind him and moved a little. *Keep kicking*, his instructor's voice echoed in his head.

Stan whirred his legs as fast as they would go. He tried moving his front legs, too, and soon he didn't need to hold on to the umbrella. He could stay afloat without it.

"I'm swimming!" he exclaimed to himself. He couldn't believe it.

Before he knew it, Stan had reached the entrance of the connecting pipe and pulled himself out of the water. He shook himself dry, wrung out his T-shirt and studied the dripping-wet map again. There was still quite a long section of pipe to follow. He just hoped he'd find Ratts and Roachy at the end of it.

Greeny-brown slime dripped from the top of the pipe, which twisted and turned as it sloped upwards. Stan slipped and slid his way forward.

Every now and again he'd encounter a stray sock, which told him he was still going in the right direction –

towards the cause of the blockage. He also found a trail of fresh chocolate biscuit crumbs, which reassured him that Ratts and Roachy had come this way before him.

At one point Stan had to jump into an adjoining pipe to avoid a big GUSH of water that came rushing past, carrying with it a big pair of ladies' bloomers. At the top of this pipe was a drain cover. He popped his head through the bars and looked up on to a street lined with human houses.

It looked a bit like the street above his bedroom.

Stan copied the street sign into his diary and wrote a very quick passage:

Dear Diary,

I'm on my own adventure!

Today I climbed a massive pile of underwear and then I actually learnt to SWIM. I still can't believe it. But there's a serious problem - I have no idea where Captain Ratts and Roachy are. I'm trying to follow the Captain's map but lots of the lines have faded after it got wet and I'm having to guess some of the directions. I'm hoping Captain Ratts has remembered where to go - so far the soggy biscuit crumbs have been my only clue.

I have to go and try to find my uncle and Roachy now. If I don't make it and someone finds this diary, please let my teacher, Mrs Scratchy, know that I did my homework.

Yours intrepidly,
Stan
(In a drain on Barrington Crescent)

Chapter 8
The Terrible Toddling Human

As Stan continued his journey, the pipes seemed to be getting narrower and slimier. He was nearing the point on the map his uncle had marked as the "final destination".

And, sure enough, as he climbed through a particularly tight bend, he could suddenly see light ahead.

Woah!

One moment Stan had been wading through a small pool of water, stunned by the bright light, the next moment he was looking over the top of . . . a human toilet seat! He scrabbled on to the shiny white rim and looked around in amazement at the vastness in front of him. He rubbed his eyes. A human bathroom!

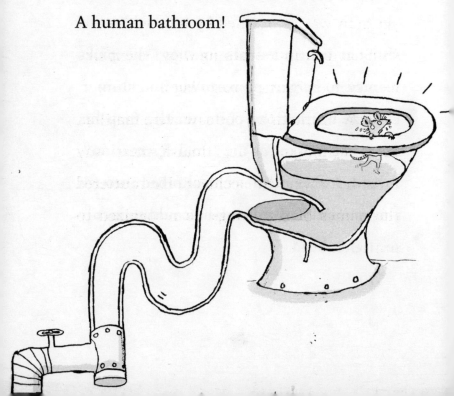

Stan had seen pictures of what human houses looked like inside at school but he'd never seen the real thing. Rats were taught to avoid the dangerous world above the sewers. A bathroom was a scary place to be – a human could capture him at any time and keep him as a prisoner, or a "pet". And yet Stan was astonished by how white and shiny and clean everything was. He felt like he was in an exotic foreign land.

Some of the things he saw were familiar. Lots of human objects found their way into the sewers by accident. He muttered the names of the things he recognized to himself.

Shampoo

Loo roll

Sponge

Rubber duck

Soap

Toothpaste and
toothbrushes

Shaving foam

"Loo roll." (A new supply for his diary!)

"Sponge." (He'd seen baby rats using these as trampolines.)

"Soap." (This didn't have much use in the sewers; rats liked to smell au naturel.)

"Rubber duck." (Stan wondered why humans liked these funny things.)

"Toothpaste and toothbrushes." (He didn't know what humans used them for, but rats liked to comb their whiskers with toothbrushes.)

"Shaving foam." (Stan had learnt this wasn't edible when some unfortunate rats in his class had mistaken it for ice cream! Mrs Scratchy told them that humans used it

because they didn't like hair on
their faces. It seemed humans were not
only bad, they were bonkers, too!)

On the floor of the bathroom was a big pile
of unwashed underwear, but it wasn't nearly
the size of the mountain down in the sewers.

Beside it was something Stan didn't
recognize, probably because it was too big
to fit down a sewer pipe. It was large and
plastic and looked like a cage. Through the
bars, Stan could see. . .

"Uncle! Roachy!"

They were trapped inside, peering out
from underneath a flannel. Their goggles
were all steamed up and they had chocolate

smeared around their faces – they must have eaten the last of their supplies.

"Stan!" cried Roachy and Captain Ratts together.

"Stay right where you are and I'll try and get you out," Stan replied. His joy at finding them made him feel brave.

"But how?" called the Captain. "Never mind. Thank goodness you're here! Roachy accidentally dropped our walkie-talkies in the river and we couldn't contact you. We're in a bit of a pickle."

"I can see that," said Stan, "but why are you hiding under that flannel?"

A monstrous sound came from somewhere outside the room, answering Stan's question.

"WAAAAAAH... WAAAAHHHH!"

The noise was so loud that it hurt Stan's ears.

"Take cover. It's coming back!" shouted the Captain.

"A human!" wailed Roachy.

Stan looked desperately around him for somewhere to hide. He jumped down from the toilet seat and made a leap for the bath, scrambling up the side as fast as his legs could carry him. He ducked behind the shower curtain just in time.

BAM!

The door of the bathroom burst open.

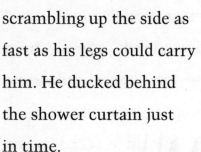

Stan sneaked a peek in time to see a terrifying giant human toddle into the room. Its mouth was stretched into a hideous one-toothed grin. It had no hair on its head and it was wearing a great big nappy (just like the ones that were currently blocking the River Gunk). Stan shuddered and watched in horror as the giant picked up a sock from the washing pile, stomped over to the toilet and deliberately dropped it in. PLOP!

Then, the huge human reached up on tiptoes, yanked down the handle . . . and FLUSHED! It giggled with delight, sending a chill down Stan's spine.

Next, the giant reached out a podgy hand and grabbed some pants.

Whoosh! Down the toilet they went.

So this was what was causing the blockage. How were they ever going to stop something as horrible as this human?

"The poor old sewer river can't take much more," the Captain whispered to Stan through the bars of his cage.

"MORE!" said the giant human, moving towards the plastic prison. The Captain and Roachy flattened themselves under their flannel.

Stan thought of some of the more random objects he'd fished out of the sewer river.

A decapitated dinosaur

A legless doll

A blind teddy

If these were the human's past victims, just think of the damage it could do to a rat or a cockroach. But Stan's worst fears were coming true – a grubby hand stretched towards Ratts and Roachy. Stan had to do something. Fast!

"Yooo-hooo! Over here!" Stan squeaked, waving his arms around. He did a brave little dance on the side of the bath.

The human spun round. **"MOUSEY!"** it shouted and lunged towards Stan.

It was like a chaotic game of cat and mouse . . . or rat and human.

Stan ran round the bathroom hiding behind one thing after another, barely catching his breath before he had to make a dash for the next safe place.

The giant human was hot on Stan's tail, bashing stuff out of the way to find him.

"MOUSEY! HERE, MOUSEY!"

Just when Stan was starting to run out of places to hide, a shout came from another room.

"Snacky time," said a loud female voice. The human stopped in its tracks, apparently forgetting all about the "fun" game it had just been playing, and toddled out of the bathroom.

"Phew." Stan collapsed on to a bath sponge and tried to get his breath back.

"Woop! Woop! Well done, Stan, that was, er . . . stupidly brave," cheered his uncle, whose eyes were wide with disbelief. "Now we need to solve this problem once and for all and get out of here before that nasty human comes back. Set us free!"

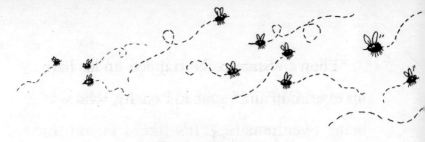

Chapter 9
Rescue from the
Cage of Doom

It wasn't as simple as it looked. The big plastic cage was too heavy to lift (even for two rats and an unusually strong cockroach using all their might). Captain Ratts' ears went bright pink with the effort.

GNNR!

GNNR

"I don't wanna to be trapped under here for ever, Cap'ain," sobbed Roachy, who was being overdramatic. "It's like a prison. In fact, I've been to prison before and they had a lot more to eat."

"Pull yourself together, man," Captain Ratts ordered. "Stan will get us out, and we've been in far worse situations. Remember our adventure with the cannibal leeches?"

Roachy nodded glumly.

Stan, who had been thinking hard, remembered something useful from one of his lessons at school: if you use a lever, you can lift heavy things easily. Mrs Scratchy would be proud, he thought to himself. He looked around for useful objects and wished he had some of the treasure junk they had tried to sell in Slime-on-the-Sewer. It would have come in handy right now. He scrambled up the sink and found a purple glittery toothbrush, and by the side of the toilet he found an empty loo-roll tube.

Balancing the toothbrush on top of the loo roll, he wedged one end under the Cage of Doom.

Stan pushed down hard on the other end of the toothbrush.

Cage of Doom →

PUSH

Loo roll

Toothbrush

The cage lifted, but just a bit.

More force was needed, Stan decided. He climbed up on to the bath and peered down at the toothbrush below him. Taking a deep breath, he ran to the edge . . . and leapt off.

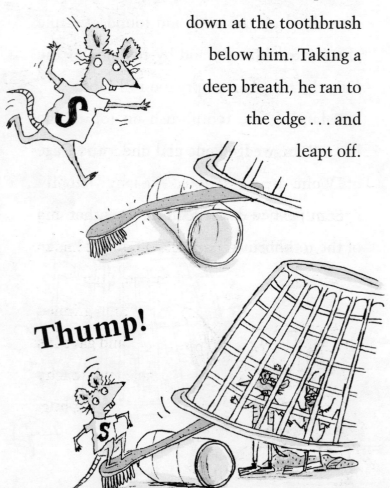

Thump!

Clunk! Clatter!

The cage flipped all the way up. "We're free!" shouted Roachy, happily jiggling his wooden leg. He took off his bobble hat and did a bow. "Thanks to you, Stan."

Stan grinned and gave his uncle and Roachy a big hug.

"WAAAAAAWAAAH! DON'T LIKE DINNER. WANT MOUSEY,"

came a wail from the room next door.

Everyone froze. It wouldn't be long before the terrible toddling human returned.

"Up to the sink for safety," commanded the Captain. "Even the Giant can't reach that high."

Sitting in the sink with the Captain and Roachy, Stan could detect the delightful, familiar smell of the sewer through the plughole. It seems so far away, Stan thought wistfully.

The Captain took out the original plan from his pocket. It was soggy and covered in biscuit crumbs.

"What's next?" he said to himself. "We've found the blockage of underwear, we know where it's coming from and now we need to stop it from appearing. Hmmm," murmured the Captain. "I can now see that our plan is not really a plan at all."

Stan rolled his eyes. He'd known this all along.

"How can we stop this human from recklessly throwing any old thing down the toilet?" the Captain mused. "Everyone THINK as hard as you can."

Five minutes later. . .

"Umm," said the Captain.

"Hmmmm," said Roachy.

"Er . . . urrr," said Stan.

Six minutes later. . .

Roachy had given up thinking and was trying to fart a tune.

And that was what gave Stan an idea. . .

He grabbed the tube of toothpaste and started to draw out his plan on the side of

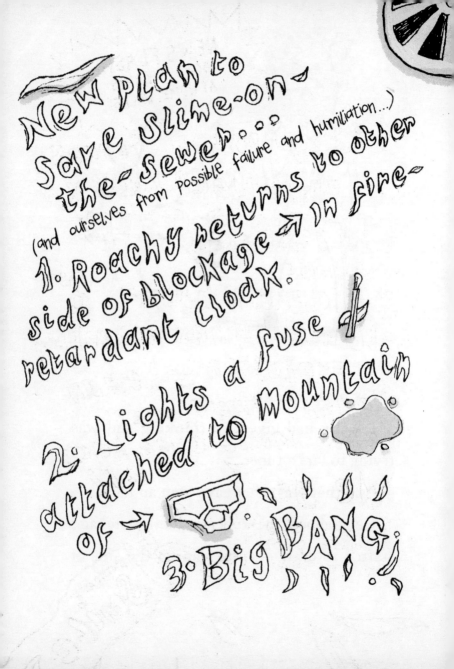

NEWS FLASH!
DON'T TRY THIS
AT HOME, FOLKS!

4. Explosion forces underwear back up pipes → (and clears blockage).

MEANWHILE:

5. Captain + Star (sing?) ♫ attract human attention to explosion = human learns what goes down must come back up!

We go home HEROES (and claim prize!).

TOOTHPASTE to SMILE

"You see?" Stan exclaimed once he'd finished writing. "Of course, me and the Captain will have to escape down the toilet after the explosion. . ."

"GENIUS!" the Captain cried, grinning from ear to ear. "My boy, you have been promoted to my Chief Adventurer."

Roachy had accidentally trod in the plan and had got toothpaste all over his legs. Stan had to explain to him that he had a crucial role, and that it involved the biggest flambéing attempt of Roachy's life. The cockroach got so excited he pulled out his harmonica and started singing and dancing.

"Gold taps! Soon to be ours. . . Precious gold taps, lovely and sparkly and—"

"Shhh," hushed Captain Ratts. "The Giant will hear. We don't want him in here yet."

Chapter 10
An Explosive Time

Ten minutes later, Stan and Captain Ratts were both perching on the edge of the toilet seat, listening intently. They had wrapped Roachy in a fire-proof cloak and had helped strap him on to a submarine device made from an empty shampoo bottle. They'd made sure that he had a large supply of matches, wrapped in tinfoil to keep them dry, and had

given him strict instructions not to light them until he was absolutely ready (which meant waiting until he was on the OTHER side of the blockage). Then, they'd flushed him down the toilet.

"Gassy winds be with you. Good luck!" shouted the Captain over the noise of the gushing water.

REMEMBER!
CHILDREN SHOULD NEVER
LIGHT MATCHES.

As Roachy whirled away down the pipe, waving his legs gleefully, Stan crossed his paws behind his back. There was still so much that could go wrong with his plan and he wasn't sure whether Roachy would actually remember what to do. He shuddered to imagine what might happen if the blockage, instead of being dislodged back up the pipe, exploded the other way towards Slime-on-the-Sewer.

"Now are we prepared?" the Captain asked.

Stan pointed to the rubber duck and the bar of soap nearby.

"Oh yes, our escape vessels," grinned the Captain. "Remember to hold on to yours tightly when we flush." He pointed to the rope they'd tied to the toilet handle. Everything was ready; they just had to wait for Roachy.

Stan thought about him down in the sewer. With any luck, the cockroach should have unstrapped himself from the shampoo bottle submarine, climbed up and through the underwear mountain and got everything ready for the detonation by now. BUT what if his journey had made him dizzy or confused?

The Captain didn't seem anywhere near as worried as Stan. He was back in "crazily

excited adventurer" mode. He kept taking
out his pocket watch and pacing impatiently
around the rim of the loo.

"I've been making calculations in my
head," he said.

"If I am correct, we should hear something happening in 5 – 4 – 3 – 2 – 1. . ."

There was silence.

Stan gulped.

Captain Ratts jostled him playfully. "That sneaky critter-roach is desperate to win those precious gold taps. He won't let us down."

And then. . .

. . . *Fizzzzzz* . . .

A noise echoed up the pipe and vibrations shook the toilet seat.

"That's our cue," shouted Stan.

He and the Captain started to sing at the top of their voices.

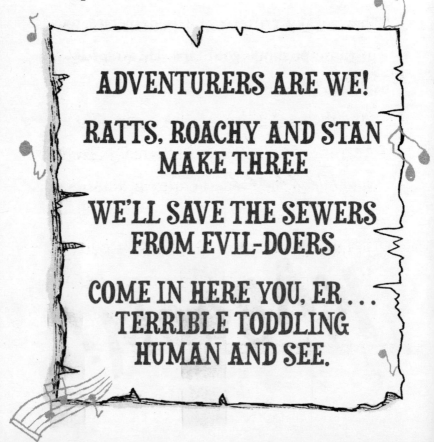

ADVENTURERS ARE WE!

RATTS, ROACHY AND STAN MAKE THREE

WE'LL SAVE THE SEWERS FROM EVIL-DOERS

COME IN HERE YOU, ER ... TERRIBLE TODDLING HUMAN AND SEE.

Their song seemed to work. From beyond the bathroom door they heard a splat and a clatter. Stan guessed it was the human throwing its dinner on the floor.

"MOUSEY PLAY AGAIN!" came a blood-curdling squeal followed by the sound of clumsy feet toddling back towards the bathroom.

Stan and the Captain were still clinging to the shaking toilet seat. The deep rumble from the pipes below was getting louder and louder.

"Blimey, we need to get out of the way. She's going to blow," yelled the Captain. They scrambled up on to the top of the cistern, just in time.

Two things happened at once:

1) Into the bathroom charged the Giant.

2) Out of the toilet blasted wet and stinky pants, socks, nappies, broken toys and quite a lot of greeny-brown slime. They splattered all over the room, sticking to the walls, the ceiling, the bath and the floor.

SPLAT! Splat! SPLAT! Splat! SPLAT!

For a moment the human just stood there looking shocked and dazed. Then, as it realized what had happened, it began to yell.

"WAAAAAAAAH! *MUMMY!"*

It was time to go.

"Ready?" called the Captain, grasping the rubber duck under one arm and diving into the toilet. Stan carefully slid in after him,

clinging to his soap and splashing around; swimming was still a new thing for him.

Just as they were about to disappear down the U-bend, another giant human marched into the bathroom, but this one was MUCH bigger than the toddling one. Its voice boomed around the room like a thunderclap.

"BARNABY! WHAT ON EARTH HAVE YOU BEEN DOING? NEVER FLUSH ANYTHING DOWN THE TOILET THAT YOU'RE NOT SUPPOSED TO. NAUGHTY, NAUGHTY BOY."

"Get set!" ordered the Captain, pulling down on the string that was attached to the flush handle.

Stan smiled to himself as he climbed on to his soap. He felt a little sorry for the smaller terrible toddling human, but he knew that no socks or pants would ever find their way into this loo again.

"GO!" cried the Captain.

Whoosh!

Stan was sucked into the toilet at great speed. It was like a super water slide. Captain Ratts was clinging happily to his rubber duck, shouting, "Woo-hoo! This is fantastic!"

Stan was finding the slippery soap a bit harder to keep hold of. He kicked his legs out behind him but that didn't make it any easier. Instead, Stan managed to grasp the soap with all four paws and sit on top of it.

And suddenly they were on the crest of a large wave down on the River Gunk. The explosion had cleared the sewer pipe and the trapped water from the other side of the underwear mountain had started to flow back to where it belonged.

Stan was swept along with the rushing water. He grabbed the sides of his soap bar and pushed himself up to a standing position. He wobbled a bit, but, with his arms out, he soon caught his balance.

"You're surfing, you salty little sea dog," cheered the Captain from his duck.

I am? I'm really SURFING! thought Stan, surprised at himself.

From the top of his wave, he saw the few stray socks and pants and the toxic gases were being washed clean away, revealing a lovely dirty brown river once more. The blockage was gone.

"Wahey! Ratabunga! We did it!" Stan cried as he surfed all the way up the river and

straight towards Slime-on-the-Sewer. A trail
of soapy bubbles popped out from behind
him. Who knew that a soap bar could make
such a great
surfboard?

Up ahead, Stan spotted Roachy and The Old Noodle bobbing up and down on another wave. Roachy was covered from head to wooden leg in grey soot and The Old Noodle was singed around the edges.

Its pants sail was smouldering slightly, but the whole thing was still floating.

"Ahoy there," Roachy called.

"Hello," waved Stan happily as he surfed past.

As he neared Slime-on-the-Sewer's harbour, Stan saw the residents were slowly emerging from their homes, blinking and breathing in the fresher air.

The Mayor was striding purposefully down the street in his ceremonial robe.

The germy-yellow smog was evaporating and everyone was discovering that the smell, although still quite strong, was now bearable without a nose peg. The flies, who had terrible headaches from all their partying, were leaving town in large numbers. Slime-on-the-Sewer was looking much more like its old self.

Many rats and bugs from all around, and even the lone pigeon, started gathering on the harbourside and embankments.

WELCOME TO SLIME-ON-THE SEWER

They watched as surges of water gushed into their nasty sticky swamp, washing away the stray underwear and transforming it back into their beloved River Gunk.

It wasn't long before the crowd spotted Stan on his slippery surfboard and they began to cheer!

Chapter 11
The Heroes Return

"They've saved the day!" Stan heard the Mayor boom into his loudspeaker.

The crowd cheered with all their might, as Stan rode a huge wave into town. Slime-on-the-Sewer's journalists and photographers pushed their way to the front of the jostling throng and started snapping and scribbling away.

There was another round of clapping and whooping as Roachy and the burnt and battered Old Noodle appeared. Finally, the crowd went wild when Captain Ratts came into view, sitting astride his rubber duck. He bowed and waved like he was king of the river.

As the wave broke, Stan tried to dismount from his soapy surfboard in a graceful manner. He ended up losing his balance and doggy-paddling around until he was heaved out of the water by a number of helpful residents.

Moments later, Stan, Captain Ratts and Roachy were standing on the harbourside, surrounded by admirers and reporters.

Stan was far too exhausted to answer any questions, so he just stood and smiled whilst the Captain, who was enjoying fame immensely, told their tale over and over again. Each time the story was told, there was more and more exaggerated drama and excitement. But the Captain gave lots of credit to Stan for the brave rescue and for being the "brains" behind the plan to save the sewers. "We couldn't have done it without him," he said.

"Three cheers for Ratts, Roachy and Stan! Hip-hip hooray," sang the crowd.

That evening, the Mayor asked the heroes to stay for a lavish banquet with the distinguished members of the Ancient Sewer Council. The menu was delicious. Roachy offered to flambé the Camembert in order to demonstrate exactly how he created the underwear explosion. The Captain seemed to forget all about his table manners and helped himself to seconds, thirds and fourths, and when he thought no one was looking, shoved extra portions into his pockets. Stan ate more than he'd ever eaten in his life.

Through mouthfuls, the Mayor told Stan how impressed he was by his surfing. He even asked Stan for some tips. "Yes, I'm not very good at swimming either; I'm more of a ballet rat myself," the Mayor admitted when Stan explained how he'd only just learnt to swim.

After dinner, Roachy's eyes lit up like saucers when the Mayor unveiled the reward of the gold taps. The Captain accepted them graciously. "Hot and cold," sighed Roachy with delight as he stroked the sparkling metal.

Me Favorit moment - ROACHy!

On The Old Noodle that night, Stan slept like a log (as did everyone else in Slime-on-the-Sewer). He was too tired to write in his diary, but the next day he devoted some time to recapping his adventure.

The Captain brought him a copy of the local paper:

CAPTAIN RATTS

and his adventure team rescue Slime-on-the-Sewer from THE RANCID UNDERWEAR MOUNTAIN DISASTER.

Terrible toddling GIANT human to blame!!!

Captain Ratts, intrepid adventurer and sewer technician, yesterday managed to restore the sewer and the River Gunk back to normality. Details of his adventure can be read on page 3.

He praised his young assistant and "chief adventurer" Stan (see surfing hero in front-page photo) for quick thinking and bravery under pressure, and the skilled pyromaniac qualities of his cockroach sidekick, Roachy.

See page 2 for the Mayor's reaction and pictures of the reward presentation.

See page 15 for many different uses for human socks and pants (there are still a few lingering in the harbour).

Stan stared at his photo. He was front-page news and, more importantly, he was surfing on front-page news!

"You've also got some post," said the Captain cheerfully, handing him two letters.

One was from his mum:

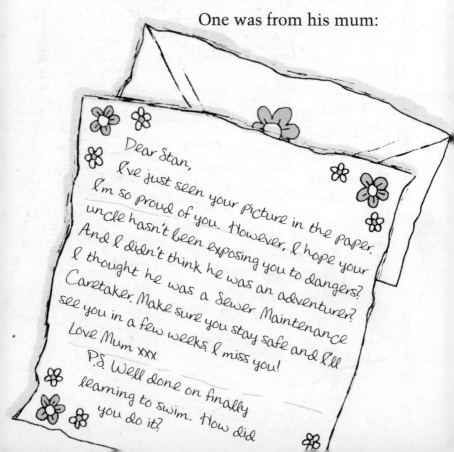

Dear Stan,

I've just seen your picture in the paper. I'm so proud of you. However, I hope your uncle hasn't been exposing you to dangers? And I didn't think he was an adventurer? I thought he was a Sewer Maintenance Caretaker. Make sure you stay safe and I'll see you in a few weeks. I miss you!

Love Mum xxx

P.S. Well done on finally learning to swim. How did you do it?

The other, Stan was surprised to find, was
from his teacher:

Dear Stan,
This is your teacher, Mrs Scratchy,
writing. I was delighted to see your face
in the paper this morning. What a tale you
will have to tell us when you return to
school! Make sure you send a postcard
to your fellow pupils in the Bahamas.
I'm sure they'd be very excited to hear
about your adventures. Looking forward
to reading your homework diary.
    All the best,
    Mrs I.A.M. Scratchy

Stan looked up from his letters to see that the Captain and Roachy were loading up The Old Noodle with supplies.

"We've sold one of the taps," explained his uncle, "and we're going to make The Old Noodle NEW again. No more patching up, no more leaks and creaks! We'll do a proper job."

Roachy heaved a box of paints on board. He didn't look best pleased about selling one of the precious taps.

"I also have a surprise," announced Captain Ratts. "We can now afford to spend a few weeks on holiday. We're going to a tropical-ish island paradise called . . . the Bananas."

THE BANANAS

"Yippee!" yelled Roachy, who was obviously over the moon.

"The Bananas?" questioned Stan. "Are you sure you've got that right?"

Chapter 12
The Bananas, or A Holiday at Last?

Dear Diary,

We've arrived in the Bananas. Which is not the Bahamas, but it's actually quite a lot like it. Except it's in the sewers and it looks a bit like this:

A plastic palm tree →

A cocktail umbrella

It has a pile of building sand on top of it

A swing →

An upside-down banana box, floating in a river backwater →

BANANAS

I'm sitting on the swing as I write, watching Roachy make cake-shaped sandcastles.

Captain Ratts has spent some time getting The Old Noodle ship-shape again. She is no longer a battered old boat. I've suggested we rename her

"The NEW Noodle"

but the Captain and Roachy are having none of it - she's still the good Old Noodle to them.

The Captain has also found the time to make me a proper surfboard from an old comb handle and Roachy has helped me paint it red with yellow stripes.

My soap surfboard has now dissolved completely. Although the waves aren't quite as good here, I can still stand up on it and paddle around.

I'm also practising my swimming. I can now swim all the way round the Bananas and I'm having a go at snorkelling too. I've managed to spot almost all of the poos on the poo chart.

Sweetcorn poo

Yesterday we took The New Old Noodle for a test sail – the pants have been patched up nicely and they've even been washed. She cruised along like a new vessel. We passed a few other tourist boats on their way to Slime-on-the-Sewer and we were surprised when they all stopped to wave and take our photos. "We saw you in the paper," they called out. Captain Ratts climbed aboard one tourist boat and dished out autographs, much to the delight of some lady dung beetles.

The Captain seemed really pleased, and when we got back to the Bananas, we had a slap-up spit-roasted worm barbecue for dinner. Later we all sat around the campfire and Roachy played the harmonica whilst we sang songs.

I only have a few more days left and then I'm going to have to go home and back to school. I'll miss having adventures and helping out. I'll miss Captain Ratts, Roachy, The Old Noodle, treasure fishing, and I'll miss sleeping in a hammock. But the Captain has promised I can come and stay with

them whenever I like. Woo-hoo! Well,
I am his Chief Adventurer, of course!

Yours unsinkably,

Stan

Before they left the Bananas, there was
much debate about what to do with the
other gold tap. The Captain said he had
enough cash left over from the sale of the
first one to keep things going for a while.
Roachy was determined to put the other
tap somewhere safe. "I say we keep it
on The Old Noodle," said the Captain.
"That way we can keep an eye on it."

"But what about thieves or pirates?" asked Roachy, looking concerned.

"Surely pirates don't exist any more?" laughed Stan.

The Captain and Roachy exchanged a look. "Maybe we should bury it?" suggested Ratts.

"Much better idea, Cap'ain," said Roachy, sounding relieved.

The Captain fetched a shovel and Roachy began digging a hole in the sand. He dug all afternoon until the hole was nice and deep. Stan helped the Captain lower the tap into the hole.

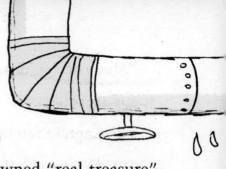

"So long, my sparkly," whispered Roachy fondly. He admitted to Stan that he'd never owned "real treasure" before. "Ah, I expect we'll be digging it up in no time," said the Captain, giving his sidekick a reassuring pat on the back.

"You never know, it might come in handy to fund our next adventure."

Stan went and sat under the cocktail umbrella and watched the Captain and Roachy cover the tap with sand. He wrote a postcard back to his friends.

• PÒSTKARTE • POSTCARD • CART

Dear all,

Sorry I haven't been in touch. It's been such a busy
summer. At first I thought I'd be bored but NO
WAY! I have been having a wicked adventure back
here in the sewers. First I learnt to swim, then I
rescued my uncle and friend from a giant toddling
human. Then I SAVED the entire town of Slime-
on-the-Sewer from an underwear disaster. Oh, and
the Mayor invited me to dinner . . . and guess what?
I have also been surfing! (See picture in *The Daily
Slime*.) Are the waves this big in the Bahamas?
Looking forward to seeing all your sunburnt faces
back at school. Can't wait to tell you more —
that's if we don't all get kidnapped by non-existent
pirates. Ha ha!
See you soon.

The now-quite-famous Stan Stinky.
(Chief Adventurer, Sewer Hero)

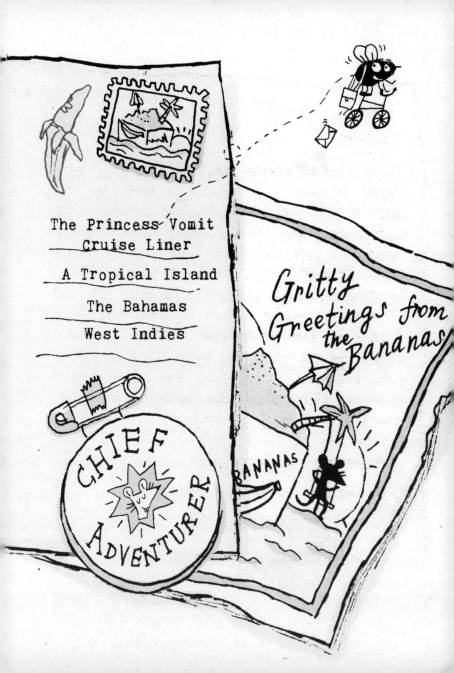

Acknowledgements

A very big squeaky thank you to my editor Alice Swan for her unparalleled support, spot-on editorial guidance and great sense of humour. Also to Alison Padley for her hard work and design prowess, and to Lucy Rogers for her helpful suggestions. Acknowledgements must also be given to my brilliant agent Penny Holroyde – for her belief that I *could* write more than a 600-word picture book! To my husband,

Ben, who not only answered questions such as "Do you think Mr Scabies is a good name for a rat?" but also put up with me moaning about my pregnant bump getting in the way of the desk. Finally, thanks to baby Meryn, who was with me all the way and timed her arrival perfectly, just after the final edit!

Thank you

20 uses for old socks

 A rat/hamster sleeping bag

A cactus cover (to prevent prickling)

A cheese cover (for keeping your Stilton moist!)

A growbag for cress

An emergency bandage

A bird feeder (fill with seeds)

An ear warmer (for horses)

A jacket-potato warmer

A dog toy (put a tennis ball in the end)

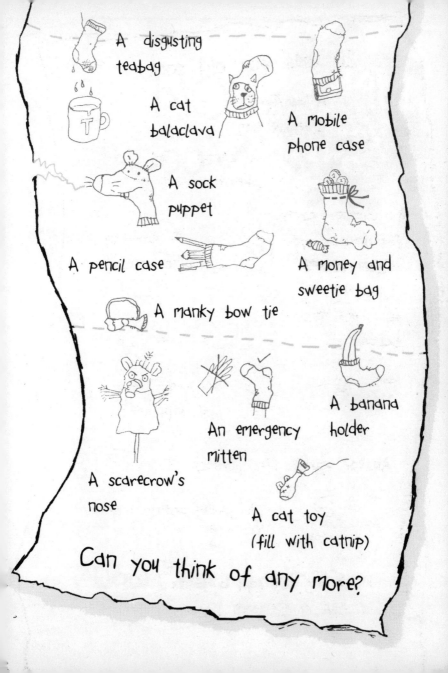

A disgusting teabag

A cat balaclava

A mobile phone case

A sock puppet

A pencil case

A money and sweetie bag

A manky bow tie

An emergency mitten

A banana holder

A scarecrow's nose

A cat toy (fill with catnip)

Can you think of any more?

Make Your Own Old Noodle

Dear human,
I hope you enjoyed my adventure.
Now how about some crafty fun?
Yours, Stan Stinky

It might even float!

You will need:

1 x big box

Munch crunch crispies crisps

2 x sticks
(These need to be tall enough to be the mast)

1 x bottle cap

1 x little box

1 x old newspaper

BORING NEWS
RAT EATS CAT

1 x tiny box

Some strong glue

A pencil/pen

A pair of scissors

A piece of paper

Parcel tape

String

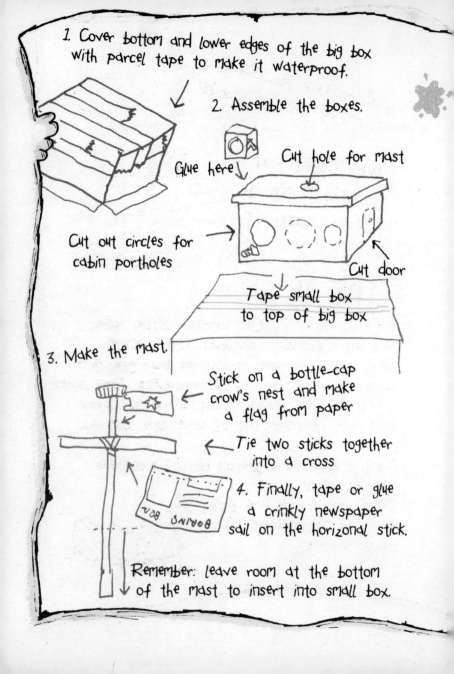

1. Cover bottom and lower edges of the big box with parcel tape to make it waterproof.

2. Assemble the boxes.

Glue here

Cut hole for mast

Cut out circles for cabin portholes

Cut door

Tape small box to top of big box

3. Make the mast.

Stick on a bottle-cap crow's nest and make a flag from paper

Tie two sticks together into a cross

4. Finally, tape or glue a crinkly newspaper sail on the horizontal stick.

BORING BOX

Remember: leave room at the bottom of the mast to insert into small box.

. . .and there you have it, your very own Old Noodle!

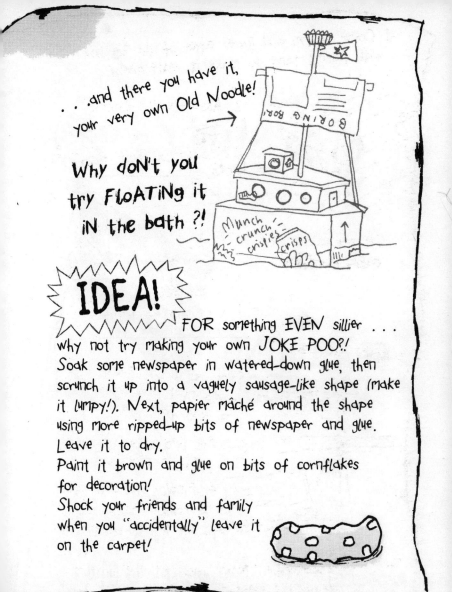

BORING BOAT

Munch crunch crispies

crisps

Why don't you try FLOATING it in the bath?!

IDEA!

FOR something EVEN sillier . . . why not try making your own JOKE POO?!
Soak some newspaper in watered-down glue, then scrunch it up into a vaguely sausage-like shape (make it lumpy!). Next, papier mâché around the shape using more ripped-up bits of newspaper and glue. Leave it to dry.
Paint it brown and glue on bits of cornflakes for decoration!
Shock your friends and family when you "accidentally" leave it on the carpet!

Look out for

Stan Stinky's

next adventure...

FEATURING PIRATES!

Coming in
summer 2014

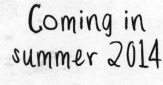

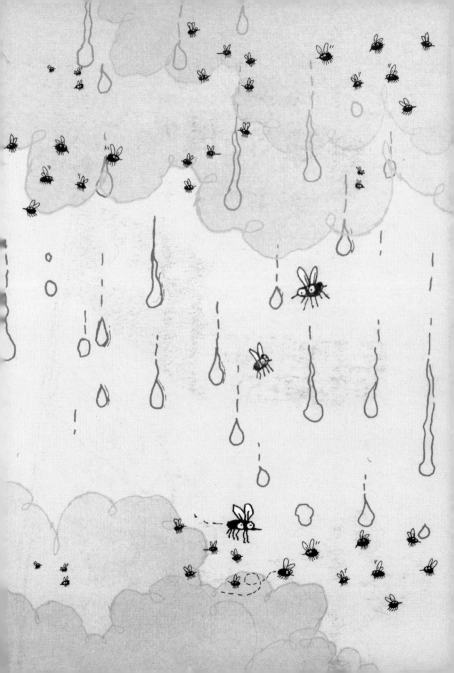

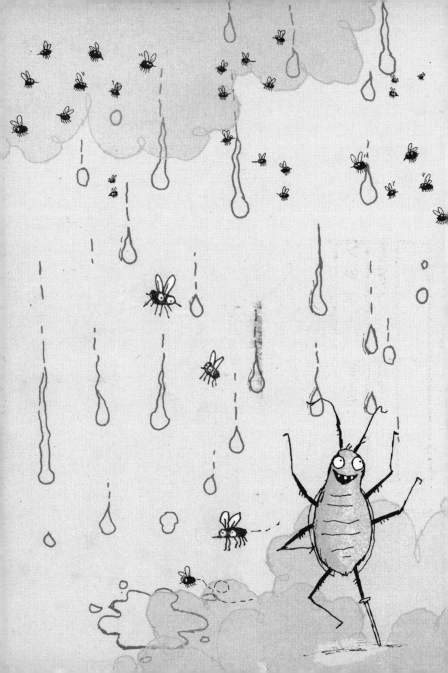